Not Just Tutus

Rachel Isadora

G. P. Putnam's Sons · New York

For Caryn

E
300- 5652

Copyright © 2003 by Rachel Isadora
All rights reserved. This book, or parts thereof, may not be reproduced in any form without permission
in writing from the publisher, G. P. Putnam's Sons, a division of Penguin Putnam Books for Young Readers,
345 Hudson Street, New York, NY 10014. G. P. Putnam's Sons, Reg. U.S. Pat. & Tm. Off.
Published simultaneously in Canada. Manufactured in China by South China Printing Co. (1988) Ltd.
Designed by Gunta Alexander. Text set in Perpetua.
The art was done in pen and ink and watercolor on Canson paper.

Library of Congress Cataloging-in-Publication Data
Isadora, Rachel. Not just tutus / Rachel Isadora.   p.   cm.
Summary: Describes the struggles and triumphs of a young girl learning and performing ballet.
[1. Ballet dancing—Fiction. 2. Stories in rhyme.] I. Title.   PZ8.3.I76 No 2003   [E]—dc21   2001008519
ISBN 0-399-23603-1
1 3 5 7 9 10 8 6 4 2
First Impression

Dreams
and Practice

Will we make it?
No one knows
Years of practice
On our toes

When I want to move
And I feel the beat
Nothing can stop me
I dance down the street

I like to leap
Across the floor
But when I land
I'm out the door

When I was little
Whenever awake
I'd dance everywhere
Till something would break

We stretch and stretch
And stretch and stretch
And then we stretch
And stretch and stretch

Nose to knees
And splits while sitting
Toes on head
You gotta be kidding

She splits and bends
What more can she do?
If she doesn't watch out
She'll break in two

My back is aching
My feet are sore
Do I want to go on?
Oh yes, I'm sure

I thought these shoes
Were soft and sweet
But man, they hurt
My little feet

Blisters, bunions
So many corns
Look at my feet
They're sprouting horns

She is thin
And she is tall
And she is pretty
They've got it all

I know that I'm short
I know that I'm round
But I want to dance
So I stand my ground

Right foot, left foot
Left foot, right
I count the steps
With all my might

Sometimes I think
I will never learn
How not to get dizzy
Doing turn after turn

I ate too much junk
And now I feel sick
It's almost my turn
Better shape up real quick

I turned around
And struck a pose
She turned left
And banged my nose

I wash my stuff
Hour after hour
Till there's no place
To take a shower

My dog ran onstage
Rehearsal was on
He did his thing
And then was gone

I hope, I hope
With all my heart
I see my name
And get the part

Makeup and Lights

It doesn't matter
If you're the best in the room
If you don't fit
Into the costume

I put on lashes
Rouge and paint
Is that me?
My mother would faint

My sister watches
What I do
She comes backstage
To make up too

If you fight backstage
Go far away
The audience hears
Whatever you say

When in costume
I must stay still
Not fuss or eat
Or drink or spill

Twinkling stars
A moonlit lake
Sometimes I
Forget it's fake

Lights go on
Curtain goes up
It's me onstage
Wish me good luck

Oh no, stage fright
I don't want to go
I'm scared but I'll smile
So no one will know

We're so young
Have far to go
But for now
We'll steal the show

The stage lights shine
Right in my face
Where's my spot?
Can't find the place

I'm onstage
All eyes watch me
But now's the time
I have to pee

Look who's leaping
In the lights
Better watch out
You're losing your tights

I'm in the spotlight
I feel all alone
I dreamed of this day
Now I want to go home

My ribbon broke
What should I do?
I must think fast
'Cause here's my cue

Applause, applause
I stopped the show
Applause, applause
I love it so

I put on wings
Just watch me fly
I turn and jump
And touch the sky

Bravo!